When Granny Saved Christmas

Julia Hubery * Caroline Pedler

LITTLE TIGER PRESS
London

"Yippeeee! It's nearly Christmas!" sang Bubble.
  "And we're going to Granny's!" added Squeak
as he helped Mummy pack his snowflake pyjamas.
  "Hurry up then," smiled Mummy, "it's a long drive!"
  "I wish we could fly to Granny's," sighed Bubble,
  "like Santa in his sleigh."

"Oh no, Bubble!" Squeak
cried. "How will Santa
know we're at Granny's?
He might come here!"

"Easy-peasy!" said Bubble.
"We'll tell him!"

"We'll scooter to Lapland,

pogo over the penguins, and hitch a polar-bear ride to the North Pole!"

"Wow, have we got time for
all that?" said Mummy.
"How about writing Santa
a letter?"

"Clever Mummy!" said Squeak
as they got to work. "Let's make
it really BIG!"

"So Santa sees it!" agreed Bubble.

With snowy sparkles and glittery glue, they made the most magnificent letter ever.

"I wrote Santa's address HUGE, to make sure it gets there," Bubble told Squeak as Daddy helped them post the letter.

But just as it plopped through the slot, Squeak cried, "Bubble! We forgot to tell Santa Granny's address. How will he know where to go?"

"I know!" said Bubble.

"We'll bake a bazillion carrotty cookies . . .

and leave a trail for Rudolph to follow!"

"Sounds yummy!" said Daddy,
as they whizzed home.
"But Granny's waiting
to see us. Could we
just leave Santa
a map?"

"Clever Daddy!" said Squeak.

Together they helped
Daddy draw a map,

and pin it to the door.

Then they helped Mummy
pack the car.

"Hooray! We're off to Granny's!"
everyone cheered, as they
squashed the boot shut.

On the way they counted Christmas trees.

"I've seen two! Six! Twenty!" yelled Bubble.

"I've seen eighty-numpty-nine!" cried Squeak.

"That's not a number!" Bubble giggled.

"It is, IT IS – isn't it, Daddy?" shouted Squeak.

"Are we nearly there yet?" sighed Daddy.

At last they saw Granny's house
sparkling in the snow.

"Grannyyyy!" yelled Bubble and Squeak,
jumping into a big Granny-hug.

"My favourite little mice!" she beamed.

Then, Bubble suddenly stopped.

"OH NO!" he gasped, staring at Granny's roof.

"Granny, where's your chimney?"
cried Bubble.

"There isn't one!" squeaked Squeak.

"How will Santa get in?"
they both wailed.

"Don't worry," smiled Granny.
"I've been very busy while I was
waiting for you. "

Bubble and Squeak followed Granny
into her garden.

"Wow!" they gasped.

"It's my Super-swishy-Santa-Slide!"
said Granny.

"Clever Granny!" cheered Squeak.

"Santa's sure to find us now!"
cried Bubble.

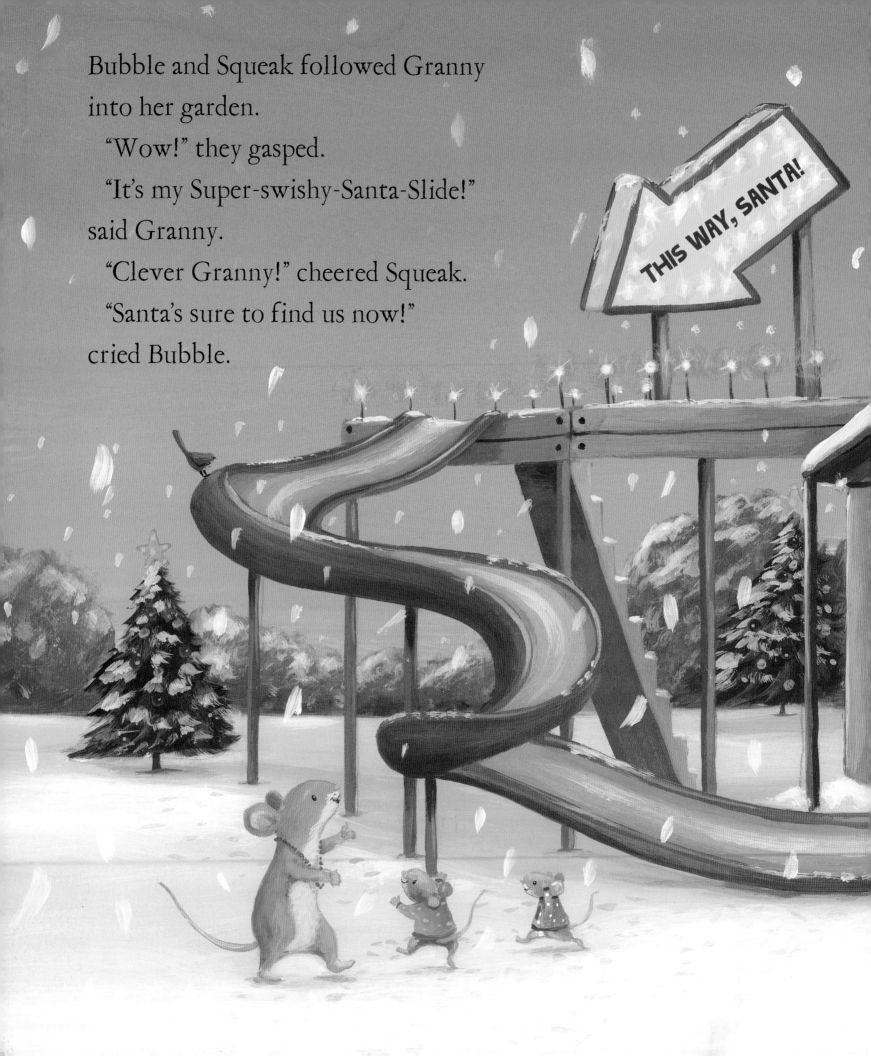

THIS WAY, SANTA!

The little mice swooped and swished down Santa's Slide until the stars began to twinkle, and Granny called, "Cocoa-time!"

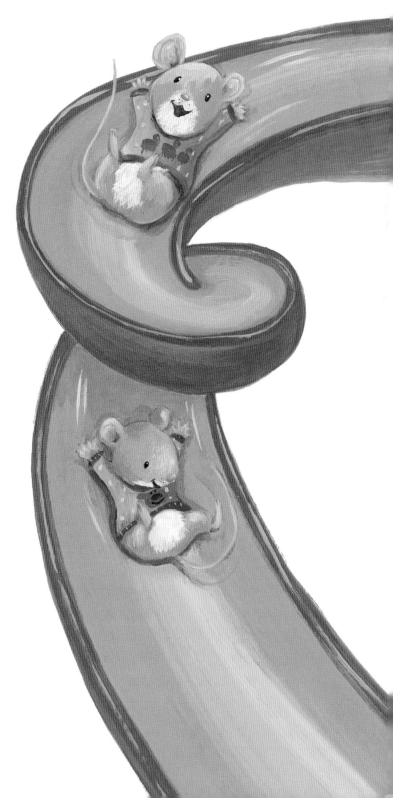

After cocoa and kisses, they wriggled
into their pyjamas, and Granny read
them a bedtime story.

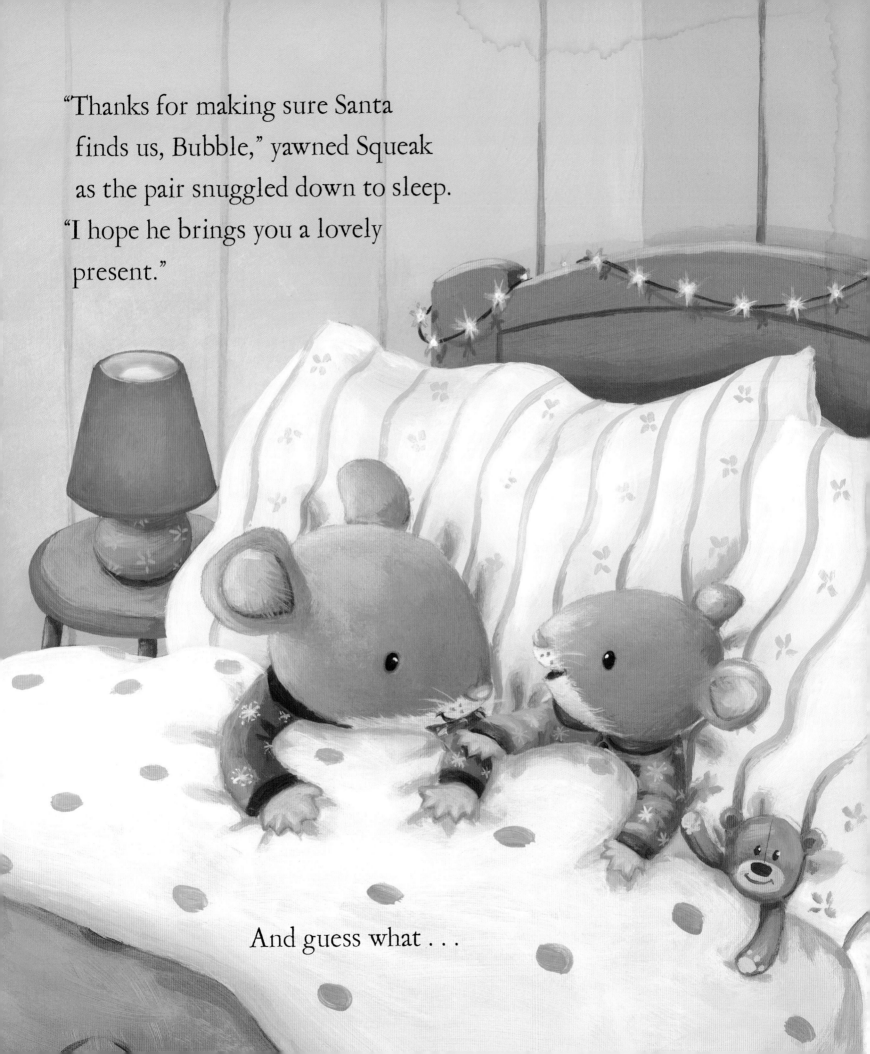

"Thanks for making sure Santa finds us, Bubble," yawned Squeak as the pair snuggled down to sleep. "I hope he brings you a lovely present."

And guess what . . .

Mum

. . . Santa did!